Hide and Snake

Hide and Snake

Keith Baker

Voyager Books

Harcourt Brace & Company

San Diego New York London

Requests for permission to make copies of any part of the work should
be mailed to: Permissions Department, Harcourt Brace & Company,
6277 Sea Harbor Drive, Orlando, Florida 32887-6777.

Voyager Books is a registered trademark of Harcourt Brace & Company.

Library of Congress Cataloging-in-Publication Data
Baker, Keith, 1953–
Hide and snake/by Keith Baker.—1st ed.
p. cm.
"Voyager Books."
Summary: A brightly colored snake challenges readers to a game of hide
and seek as he hides among familiar objects.
ISBN 0-15-233986-8
ISBN 0-15-200225-1 pb
[1. Snakes—Fiction. 2. Picture puzzles. 3. Stories in rhyme.]
I. Title.
PZ8.3B175H1 1991
[E]—dc20   90-19967

G F E D C

Printed in Singapore

The illustrations in this book were done in Liquitex acrylics on
illustration board.
The display type was set in ITC Zapf International Medium Italic.
The text type was set in Zapf International Medium.
Composition by Thompson Type, San Diego, California
Color separations by Bright Arts, Ltd., Hong Kong
Printed and bound by Tien Wah Press, Singapore
This book was printed on Arctic matte art paper.
Production supervision by Warren Wallerstein and Ginger Boyer
Designed by Michael Farmer

Ready or not—here I go!

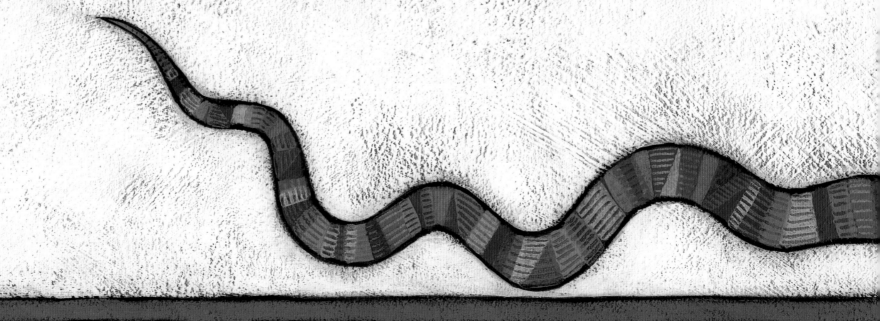

I'm looping through yarn,

curling 'round hats,

and napping  with cats.

I'm frosting the cakes,

ticking with clocks,

melting in ice cream,

and sliding through socks.

I'm playing with toys,

twisting 'round vases,

weaving through baskets,

and tangling with laces.

in so many places!

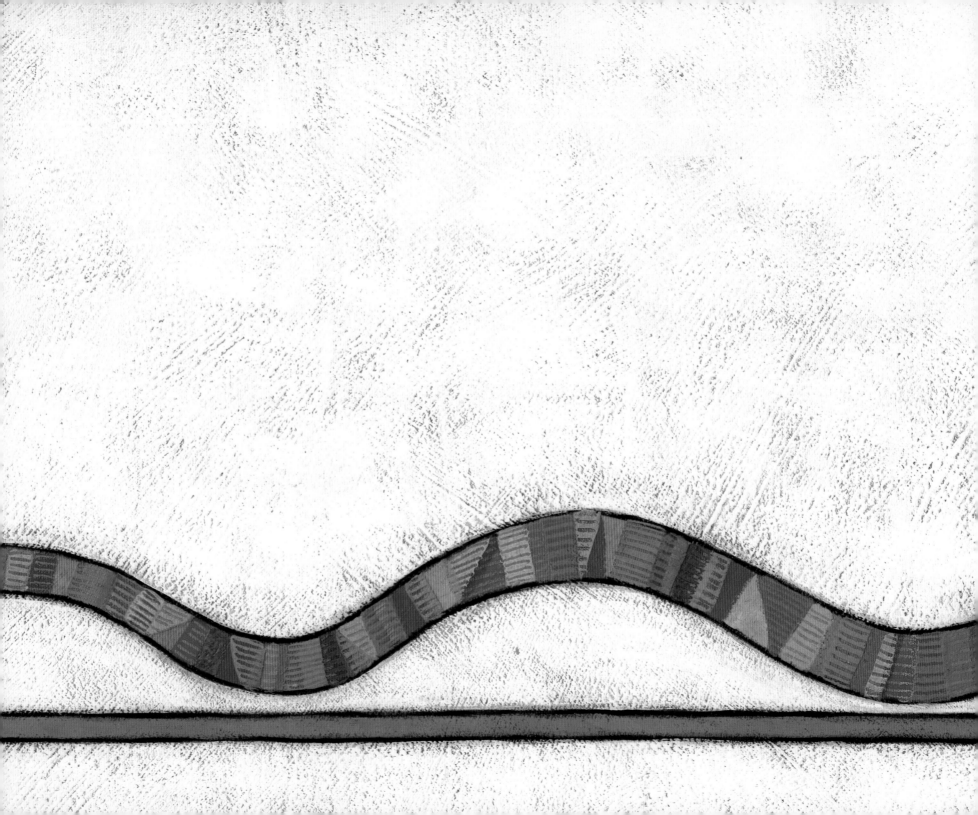

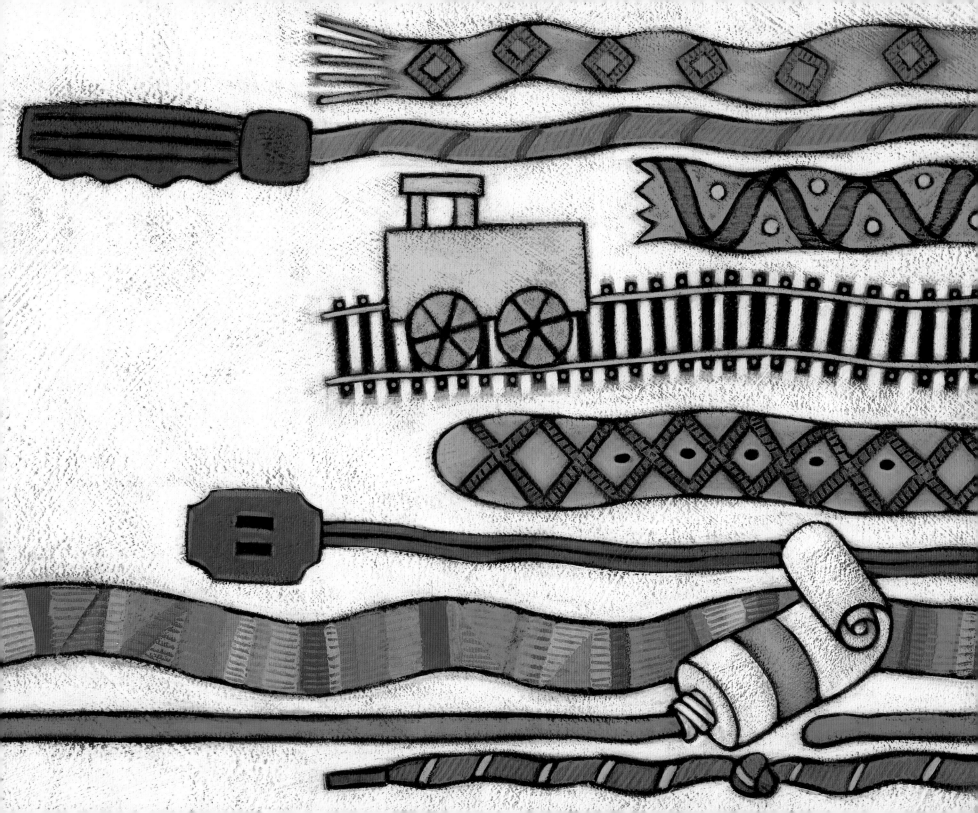